COUNTERATTACK

AMANDA HUMANN

MINNEAPOLIS

Darby Creek
A division of Lerner Publishing Group, Inc.
241 First Avenue North
Minneapolis, MN 55401 U.S.A.

Website address: www.lernerbooks.com

Main text set in Janson Text LT Std 55 Roman 12/17.5
Typeface provided by Adobe Systems

The images in this book are used with the permission of:
Front cover: © Chris Crisman/CORBIS. iStockphoto.com/
Ermin Gutenberger, (stadium lights).

Humann, Amanda.
        Out of sync / by Amanda Humann.
        p.   cm. — (Counterattack)
        ISBN 978–1–4677–0304–8 (lib. bdg. : alk. paper)
        [1. Soccer—Fiction. 2. Best friends—Fiction.
    3. Friendship—Fiction.] I. Title.
    PZ7.H8882Cla 2013
    [Fic]—dc23   2012021987

Manufactured in the United States of America
1 – BP – 12/31/12

TO TORI, TOM, JESSICA,
TAD, AND JAY AND AUNT
MARLENE—YOU ARE THE BEST
FANS A PLAYER CAN HAVE.

"a winner is that person who gets up one more time than she is knocked down."

■ ■ ■

MIA HAMM

chapter 1

sprint toward number 29, a tall redhead from the opposing team. As I prepare to steal the ball, closing the gap between 29 and me, I glance at the sidelines again. And then 29 zips past me. I'm looking for my best friend, Dayton Frey, who plays right forward and hasn't shown up yet.

Luckily, our defense is pretty strong. One of the defenders boots the ball back up to our left forward, who dribbles it toward the goal.

We haven't scored yet, but that should change ASAP.

29. ASAP. My whole life is a series of letters and numbers. Some I love, like AC and OJ. Those are necessities in North Carolina—something to cool you off, something to drink. I also love 26 (my jersey number for the last five years and the number of bones in the human foot), and my middle name, 8. As in Madison 8 Wong. Not spelled out but as an actual number. Mom insisted that my name contain the luckiest Chinese number, and Dad went with it.

Some letters and numbers I just gotta live with, like ENG II, CHEM I, SAT, and the NCAA, all of which affect my chances of getting into a good college.

And then there are some letters I just don't know what to do with, like my BFF, who is MIA. Dayton and I have been playing soccer together on the same teams since we were six. Our passes to each other are perfect. It's like we read each other's minds. Our teammates on the Fleet Feet Premier U-17 Soccer Club team and the Fraser High School soccer team, the Copperheads, call it "sick soccer sync."

Today was supposed to be our chance to show that sync to college recruiters at the December Club Soccer Showcase in Raleigh, a short drive from our hometown, Fraser.

Mostly, the National Collegiate Athletic Association's Division I soccer recruiters start looking at players in their sophomore year. Nita Ortiz, a junior at school and the star striker on both my club and school teams, started getting recruiter attention when she was a freshman. I hoped some of her limelight would shine on me and Dayton at the showcase. But for the first time in three years, Dayton hasn't shown for a club game. And I *need* her for the sync. Nobody will notice me otherwise. I'm like an island at center midfield.

I keep checking the sidelines, but there's still no sign of Dayton. She's been late before, but the first half of our game is almost over.

The opposing goalie deflects our left forward's shot. I manage to take possession of the ball and scan the field for open players.

"Nita!" I yell as I feint to the left and pop the ball over the nearest defender. I look for Dayton one more time as my toe scoops up and sends the ball up to Nita.

Only the ball isn't headed her way because the player I sent the ball to isn't Nita.

In fact, she isn't even on my team. *Fail.*

▦　▦　▦

Failure isn't an option with the sync. The best game our club had this season was when we beat the Spring Valley FC U-17 Grizzlies. It was mostly due to Dayton and me—the team within the team. After an uneventful first ten minutes, our team got into the groove and started slamming balls at the goal. Despite the chilly weather, Dayton and I were on fire.

Near the end of the half, I shot the ball between a defender's legs, sensing Dayton was right behind her. Dayton trapped it and played it at the goal past another defender. Like bear fishing for salmon, the Grizzlies keeper swatted at the ball, but it sailed straight through her clumsy mitts.

At the kickoff, Dayton got the ball and we pushed it forward, passing it back and forth with one touch. I didn't look on the last pass. I knew Dayton was exactly where she should be—to the right of the goal, dodging defenders without stepping offside.

She fired the ball at the goal, but it smashed the base of the goalpost and bounced right back at me in front of the goal. I tapped it with my knee, and it went in. The play happened so quickly that the goalie was still at the other corner.

"Slinky sync! You guys rock!" Nita yelled as we ran back for the next kickoff.

Dayton got three more shots on goal from our sync though none of them made it in.

The Spring Valley midfielders started to play back, helping the defenders cover Day and me. We had a harder time getting around them, but we still found spaces in between. At the end of the first half, we got the ball to Nita, who nailed a hard instep kick that the goalie touched but couldn't stop, making the score 3–0.

In the second half, the Grizzlies threw more and more players at us on the right side of the field. It was getting crowded, so our team shifted play to the left. Nita put another goal in, and Spring Valley clumped around her after that. The Grizzlies managed to boot the ball forward a few times and even made one solid goal, but that's all they got.

After the next kickoff, I stole the ball from their midfielder. Dayton and I danced around the defenders on us, shifting left or right at the same time so that we had clear paths to pass. Back and forth, we passed it to each other in a synchronized soccer waltz. Shift, dribble, dribble. Pass, dribble, dribble.

When we got in deep, Dayton pounded the ball and it zipped into the goal over the goalie's leg. Five minutes before the end of the game, we did it again.

When we finished, the score was an unbelievable 6–1. Our sync was responsible for two-thirds of the goals.

But there was no sync today at the showcase.

▩ ▩ ▩

After the showcase game, I texted Dayton, but only after I got a rousing pep talk from Nita: "What were you thinking?" over and over with different emphasis each time. "*What* were you thinking?" "What *were* you thinking?" "What were you *thinking*?" I also got a few long looks from some other players. Good thing that we won and that it's the last club game we'll play until summer.

As I wait for Dayton to reply, all I can think of is my chance at getting into a Division I soccer school like Stanford or Duke circling the drain. I've never had much playing time without Dayton on the field, and my game got even worse after the bad pass. I was relieved when I got subbed out. At least on the sidelines, I couldn't make any more mistakes.

Sitting out also gave me lots of time to watch for Dayton, get super pissed, and then feel sick that a recruiter may have noticed my pathetic pass. I finally managed to cool off when I realized she just wasn't coming.

Where R U sync sister? I texted her.

chapter 2

"So where were you?" I say to Dayton when she plops down in the chair next to me. Whoops, I'm not fully cooled off after all.

We're waiting for the first meeting of our soccer club's recruiting consultant sessions to start. It's always held on the same day as the last showcase game.

"Jeez, Mad Dog. Chill," says Dayton. Her voice is raspy as if she's been gargling gravel.

"I got sick this morning after Mom and Dad left to take Krystina back to UNC. Let me tell you—there is nothing grosser than puking up last night's Krispy Kremes at six in the morning."

"That sucks," I say. "Shouldn't you still be at home?"

Dayton lowers her voice and tilts her head toward my shoulder. "I'm not *sick* sick. Remember how Krys gave me her old fake ID for Christmas? I went out last night with her and some of her friends. I've got a killer hangover."

"Before a showcase game?" I find myself channeling Nita. "What were you thinking?"

"I didn't realize how bad it was going to be."

She looks so miserable that my crankiness level lessens. This is the Dayton that I know and love. She is the friend who shares a passion for soccer with me and would have been at my side any other weekend.

Just then, the head recruiting consultant, Marta, starts the session overview. "The order of your life, if you are serious about Division I soccer, is simple," she says. "Family, school, soccer practice, games, training, and recruiting."

She points to a chart showing a pyramid with these things stacked in order. "Hanging out with friends, video games, the Internet, and TV all come after those top things are taken care of."

Dayton stops writing in her notebook and just stares at it. I hope she's not going to puke.

"Most college soccer recruiting is done by the end of the junior year of high school," Marta goes on. "The bigger Division I schools start formal contact at the end of the junior year. If you're really good, they've been looking at you as freshman and sophomores.

"Your job as sophomores is to research schools, focus on grades, and improve your level of athletic ability. Recruiters don't really watch high school games, so you should also think about what club team you play for. Your overall club is well known, but some of your teams do more traveling than others and get more time in front of recruiters."

I look sideways at Dayton. She's seriously pale, and she's closed her eyes.

"This summer, you should try out for the ODP team—that's Olympic Development Program. Also, invites will be coming out in spring for D-1 camps, and you should be doing those too. Coaches don't really scout for new players at camps. They watch the players who are on their lists already. But performance is still everything. If you have a bad day playing, you might be dropped from a coach's list of possibilities."

I feel prickles all over my skin as I remember this morning's game. And she's not done.

"Very few high school players are actively recruited. You have to recruit yourself." She talks about how we can contact recruiters even if they can't contact us yet, and she goes over how we should practice gathering video clips of our play.

It's a lot to digest, and by the time we get

a break, I have ten pages of notes and a long list of goals and to-dos. Dayton has three lines scribbled in her notebook. She must feel awful.

"I'm so sorry you missed the game," I say. "The best part was that Nita dyed the tips of her hair Tar Heels blue last night in case a UNC scout was in the stands."

Dayton rasps out a weak laugh. "Wish I could've seen that!"

I want to tell her about how much I needed her there and that I'm glad to hear she was planning on showing up.

"At least you got to play in some of the games," I say. "Too bad that you missed the one game where Nita recognized a recruiter. It was one of Krystina's coaches." Dayton is silent, staring at her cup of punch.

Dayton's older sister, Krystina, plays for UNC Chapel Hill. I was going to let Dayton know that Nita also thought she saw the coach from Duke too, but I figure Day must feel pretty bad already. I'm probably making it worse telling her she's missing out on recruiter action. Either that or the silence means she's going to barf again. Some best friend I am. I change the subject again to something else she really likes.

"Do you need anything? Want a box of Frankenberry?" I ask. "I think you left a box in my car on Thursday. I can go get it."

"Yeah, cereal would be awesome. Wait." She turns pale and grabs her stomach. "Uh-oh. Krispy Kremes are back." She walks away quickly. When she turns the corner in the hall, I can hear her running for the bathroom. Gross. I try not to think too hard about it. My own stomach still feels a little queasy from picturing a recruiter putting a big, black line through my name on the "to-watch" list.

When Dayton returns and says she's going home, I'm not surprised. At least, I know now that she would totally have been there for us this morning. And there are still our regular soccer season games to work on skills and get in shape for club stuff next summer. All is right with the world.

chapter 3

"Okay, seriously, I don't think that the next Women's U-17 World Cup player should be on film burping up Cheerwine soda behind the bleachers." I move the camera away as Dayton lets loose another huge belch and starts laughing.

It's almost the end of winter break, and we need to get some footage for our recruiting highlight videos. We came out to the field at school in full uniform to get some shots of us playing. I lean around the tripod and fiddle with the camera controls to erase the burp scene. "Will you be serious?"

"I fell kind of hard on that scissor kick. I couldn't help it. It just bubbledy-bubbed up." She rubs her legs and tucks her head down to her chest, smiling. "Dude, it's so cold out here. People are totally gonna notice our breath coming out in clouds and that there are no other players on the field. I know I owe you but really. This is so not gonna work. Vacation's almost over. Let's do something fun. Please, Maddie?" She gives me puppy dog eyes.

"We got some good clips of me, but you still need some," I say. "Aren't you worried? I *totally* am. My New Year's resolution is to get back on track with my grades and the whole recruiting thing."

Dayton just looks at me. Finally, she says, "My resolutions, *if I made them*, would be to have more fun and get you to loosen up. What are you worried about? You can afford to go anywhere. It's not like you're Nita and need a scholarship just so you can go to school. Don't you ever just want to live in the moment?"

I turn the camera off and glare at her. "I have to get on a college team just to get into a school. A *good* school. My grades are not going to get me in anywhere right now, and I am terrified of the SAT. I suck at tests. Soccer's my ticket in."

"You're right. You're right. Still it's not gonna hurt you to chill out a little," she says, giggling and juggling the ball from foot to foot. I think it would be great for the video, but before I can turn the camera back on, she's done. I shiver as I realize that it *is* cold out here.

"Fine, I give up. We can get your footage some other time. What do you want to do?"

⁛ ⁛ ⁛

After telling the cute guy at Stuff on a Stick at the mall that I do indeed want it dipped in nuts, I regret letting Dayton pick our activity. At the other end of the counter, she flips her

23

hair over one shoulder and smiles brightly at the cuter guy behind the counter. He hands her a frozen banana on a stick and a little piece of paper with a wink.

"I can't believe that guy gave you his number. Kind of old school, but he's totally your type," I say as we walk away.

"It wasn't just his number. It was a time and date."

I stop mid-nibble. "You mean, you got a date just from ordering a frozen banana? No wonder it took you so long to order."

"Yup. They want to meet up with us at . . ." she opens the little piece of paper, ". . . ten on Friday night at Sugar Mill in Raleigh. Yay! Krys says that club is totally party rockin'."

I sigh. "I can't go. I have to finish that book for my English II class that I was supposed to read over break. Besides, you're the only one with the spiffy new fake ID."

Dayton pouts. "Crap, I totally forgot you need an ID."

"Yeah, and I don't have a look-alike sister in college who'll give me her old ones like

Krystina does with you." Dayton pulls the ID out, and we look down at it.

"You are so lucky, Day. You look like her, you both love soccer, not to mention you're both insanely good at it. I wish someone else in my house played."

"Yeah," she says quietly. "Lucky. But we aren't totally alike." Then Dayton actually scowls. "I don't *love* soccer. That's her. And you."

I'm confused. "How can you not *love* it? You're so good at it! Why would you keep playing if you didn't?" And then I get it. "Oh, you *totally* love it. You're just mad that I can't go out with you and the banana boys on Friday." Dayton's getting that cranky look she gets when she doesn't want to admit something. I poke her in the side with my empty banana stick. "Come on, admit it."

She frowns. But after another poke with the stick, a smirk breaks through. "Whatever. Since you'll be dating a book on Friday, you're not going to get all pissed if I take Brianna with me, instead?"

I would be sad, but I have no right to be. Brianna, who plays right D on our school team, is the perfect friend for any boy adventure. Guys love her. And if anyone else has a fake ID, it's Bri.

"Nah," I say. "Go for it. But you better be up for a little run on Saturday morning. Now that club season is over, we can't get all flabby waiting for school soccer season to start in February." I dodge the chunk of banana Dayton tosses at me with a smile. Once again, everything is okay.

chapter 4

A few weeks into January, my workload and stress level triple. Training for spring soccer (yay!), homework (boo!), and researching Division I schools (yay again!) would have been enough. Then I decided my college and recruiting résumés needed extracurricular activities, so I volunteered for the Service to Seniors club. And I added an SAT prep course. I think I can handle it, because everything seems to be going great.

Well, except for one thing. I hardly ever see Dayton. We don't have classes together this semester. I'm getting lonely. It seems like the only time I see her is during lunch at school or when I can convince her to train with me for soccer. To my surprise, that doesn't happen very often.

Dayton is known for being the most gung ho, up-for-anything player on our club team. Last summer, we played the Rickleton Inferno rec team for a scrimmage. A lot of players were upset when Coach decided to have us try different positions for the game. They complained that we should each be doing what we do best to show the difference between rec and premier teams.

But not Dayton. She was thrilled to play left defender. She spent hours practicing tackles and trying to play long-ball style.

When we got to the field, I was in at sweeper. It started raining, and a large mud puddle formed in front of the goal box. The Inferno striker dribbled around the puddle instead of through it, which meant she kept heading right for Dayton. Dayton stopped her every time.

On the fifth attack, the striker pivoted in front of Dayton and tried to pass the ball off. But it stalled in the puddle. I barreled through the water and muck, lifted the ball with my toe, and heaved it over to Dayton. She got under it, ignoring the sloppy drops of mud spinning off, and headed it over the Rickleton striker. Then, in a burst of speed, she sprinted up field. Trapping the ball, she dribbled forward and dropped her shoulder into a Matthews turn, curving around the Infernos' right forward. The Rickleton midfielders were still trying to catch up when Dayton sent a long ball to the other end. Our left forward got it and pelted it at the goal. The ball eked under the keeper's ribs and into the net.

Not being afraid to get filthy was our winning strategy, and Dayton's mix of offensive skills and killer D moves meant Rickleton couldn't score from her corner. When we won the game 1–0, we celebrated with a mud fight.

I'm sitting in the lunchroom reliving the Rickleton game in my head when Dayton comes in for our daily powwow. Instead of the female soccer player's unofficial "off-duty" uniform of ponytail, T-shirt, and sweats, she is wearing skinny jeans and a cute top I've never seen before. She flips her loose hair over her shoulder, grinning as she waves to two junior guys I don't know.

"Who are they?" I ask as she sits down and pulls open a mini box of Corn Pops.

"Those are the guys I texted you about on Friday, remember?" She pulls out a handful of cereal and starts to pick at it piece by piece.

I remember getting a confusing text from her that night. It said *ht gys. gp. U har nw.* Mystery solved.

"Text, huh? You mean this one?" I show it to her, and she almost blows Corn Pops all over my ham sandwich.

"That's awesome—it's sooo bad! I thought it was tons of lines. I described each guy and wrote that you'd like the one with the dark hair. Ha!"

I glance at the guy, and she's right—he's hot—but I have other things on my plate.

"So I ran into Nita the other day when I was out on my run."

"Yeah, sorry I couldn't make it," she mumbles.

"No big deal," I say. "Anyway, Nita's thinking of switching club teams." Dayton looks at me with a blank face. "I was thinking that we should get some extra practice in with her now in case we lose her as a teammate this summer."

She doesn't say anything, just chews. Once she swallows, she says, "Sounds like a lot of work."

"Yeah, but we'd get more practice for our sick soccer sync."

"It sounds kinda lame when you say that out loud." She grimaces. "We can't call it that. Only other people can call it that."

"Okay . . . but if we want to get any higher level experience, we need to up our game."

She sighs and shakes the box of cereal. "Why are you saying 'we'? I'm not sure that I want . . . I just . . ." She sits back and looks at me sadly. "Let's talk about something else right now, okay? Let's just enjoy our break from soccer before practice starts this afternoon."

Her eyelids droop, her hair's messy, and she just looks . . . tired. I suddenly realize she probably has the same problem with her schedule that I have, and I feel a surge of pity. As hard as this Division I recruiting thing is for me, it must be harder on Dayton. She's always been more of a free spirit.

"I get it. A break," I say, nodding.

She looks so relieved that I can almost feel it.

"Great," she says, smiling. She perks up. "So what do you think about joining me on a future Friday for a little outing? Bri and I had the best time at Sugar Mill, but I missed you. I figured if I asked you now, you can fit it in your schedule, and we can work on getting you an ID."

I know the homework won't stop, and every week I address letters for the Service to Seniors Club, but I'll have to join her sometime.

"Okay, I'll bite."

chapter 5

should have known when I bit the noodle in half that I was in trouble. During my family's Chinese New Year dinner, I accidentally bit a long-life noodle short. According to my mom, this can mean all sorts of things—less luck, a broken relationship, and even (duh) a shortened life. Since the dinner, I've been following my mom's advice and wearing the lucky color red. Even so, my luck seems to be fading.

I'm behind in two of my classes. I got a bad score on the first practice test in the SAT prep course. Copperheads' preseason practice started today. And Dayton is MIA again. Not physically but mentally.

We're out on the field doing drills, and I might as well be here alone. I know she's been spending more time keeping up socially than keeping up her soccer skills. I'm not surprised when she actually misses the first three passes I send her during give-and-go drills. By the fifth pass, I realize we're totally out of sync.

"First, you forget your shin guards," I start. "Now you're missing passes like you're dodging some creeper at a party. What's up?"

She gives me a half smile and fusses with her laces. "I'm just kind of tired and . . . not into it today."

"Seriously? Being on varsity last year doesn't guarantee a spot this year. Thank God, recruiters don't pay much attention to high school play. You'd be dead."

Dayton laughs, takes the ball, and says, "That might be a good thing. I'd have more time to just hang out. Though I dunno who I'd hang with. I never see you except for soccer stuff."

"I know. This was all way easier last year before the recruiting thing."

Coach Berg blows a whistle and all drills stop. "Copperhead one touch!" he yells.

Everyone picks pairs, and we start distance passing the ball back and forth using only one touch. Each single touch gets a letter from *Copperhead*. Dayton can barely get beyond *Cop*. She just stops trying, even pausing and holding the ball when Coach's back is turned. I don't want to get her in trouble, so I don't say anything. I just gesture. A lot.

But when the boys' soccer team comes around the corner of the field on a run, Dayton's back. It's like someone flipped a switch. She pops that ball right back at me with clean, controlled kicks.

"Woo-hoo!" she yells every time she sends the ball back to me. She dances. She jogs in place. The sync is working, except she keeps scoping out the boys as they go by.

I'm so thrilled she's playing for real that I don't care about her attempts to get attention. Her focus on soccer lasts for the remaining practice. When we get grouped with Nita to play "Outnumbered," we only have to do push-ups twice when we can't get the ball away from her. This is saying a lot, since Nita has the best ball control of anyone in the league.

"I swear you're the reason I have decent upper body strength, Nita," Dayton says in the locker room after practice.

"You wouldn't need me to whip you into shape, chica, if you lay off all that junk you eat." She grimaces at the snacks in Dayton's orange soccer duffel bag. "You'd have so much more energy if you ate healthier. Try this."

Nita offers Dayton a brown granola bar.

"Does it have chocolate chips?" Dayton asks.

"No."

"Dried fruit or sweetened nuts?"

"No."

"Artificial food dyes, trans fats, or artificial sweeteners?"

"God, no."

"No thanks, then. And good thing it's high school soccer season. If my Cheerwine gets replaced with spring water in the Fleet Feet cooler again, someone's gettin' hurt."

Nita shakes her head. "Food is fuel. We need quality fuel to play well. Want to work that junk food off with a little extra practice this Friday night?"

"Sure," I say, just as Dayton says, "Nah. I gotta go."

I don't understand what Dayton's thinking. This is a chance to sharpen her skills. Is her schedule overwhelming too? Is it homework? And then I remember I was going to go out with her and Bri this Friday.

I totally forgot. I even let a paper for English and studying for my chemistry test slide, thinking I had all weekend including Friday to catch up. I wait for her to say something, but she doesn't. As she edges away toward the door, I can feel her slipping away from me too. I don't think. I just react. "Oh, I totally forgot—we're going out on Friday. Right, Day?"

Dayton smiles slowly and then nods.

"Okay," says Nita, picking up her bag and heading for the door. "If you want to do it some other time though, let me know. And don't forget your sophomore club recruiting review night is the same day as our first Copperhead game. A whole day of soccer! It's like heaven!"

She's out the door before I can respond, but Dayton manages to mumble, "Right. Heaven." And then she's gone, ASAP.

chapter 6

We haven't had our first game yet, and I'm already exhausted. I managed to keep it going until I started making an effort to have it all. "All" meaning good grades, good practice SAT scores, good efforts at soccer practice, and good attendance at the Service Club. It's already a lot, and that's without straining to include a social life because I'm worried about losing my best friend.

"I'm so stoked Krystina found you an ID.

This rocks," says Dayton, shivering with me and Bri outside in line at the Sugar Mill. She and Bri are wearing backless tops, and she lent me a short skirt and stilettos—in February.

Krys has a friend who kind of looks like me and persuaded her to lend me an old driver's license. For the night, I am Jennifer Nishito, college student. Japanese heritage, black hair, five foot four, and living in Chapel Hill. I repeat this to myself a few times.

If it weren't so cold, I'd be sweating. I try not to imagine getting caught and possibly screwing up my entire future. All I want to do right now is be with my best friend. It felt weird over the last two months—not being around each other as much as we were during the club soccer season. I keep telling myself tonight is for the best.

The bouncer at the door barely glances at my ID as he flicks his flashlight over it. He waves us all in.

Inside, I'm overwhelmed by a sweet and smoky scent and the music blasting out of huge speakers. The bass thumps up through my stilettos and into my rib cage. It feels like it's taking over my heartbeat. I inhale and try to sort out the scene.

The Sugar Mill is (surprise!) in an old sugar mill. Tall, narrow, and open in the middle, it's like being in a grain silo. The dance floor and bar are on the main floor. Tiered balconies with open metal stairs spiraling between the levels cover the sides. Every straight edge is lined with rope lights.

For a second, I stand and stare until Dayton laughs. She leans in to talk closer to my ear.

"Nice, huh? Now be cool, or we're gonna be totally outed as high school girls." I'm still speechless, so I just stand at her side while she orders drinks.

"Heeyy!" Bri yells to some guys at the bar, who walk over to us. They are clean-cut and better groomed than most boys my age. I wonder if they're in college—or older. Dayton does the introductions. I can barely hear her above the noise of the place, so I don't catch anyone's name.

There are three of them. Day and Bri each pick a guy and head for the dance floor, leaving me with number three. He's cute, but he seems old, and looks like he's barely able to stand. I'm a little freaked out as I sip my drink. I crane my neck around him, looking for my friends.

I'm so out of my comfort zone. Day briefed me earlier on the basics before we came. No drinks from guys. Keep any drink with you at all times with your hand over the top. Tell each other where you're going to be, so you can watch out for one another. My heart jumps in double time to the beat until I spot Dayton's blonde mane in the crowd.

The guy asks me to dance. At least I think he does, since he says something and drags me to the dance floor. I barely have time to let go of my empty cup. Thankfully, we end up next to the other girls. I feel comfortable enough that I move a little more and even start to enjoy myself. I move around with Dayton and Bri as we dance more with one another than the guys.

Dayton dances over to me with a smirk and asks how it's going. I think. The beat still dominates my hearing, so I just nod and smile.

Five or six songs have gone by when Dayton, all sweaty and glowing, grabs Bri's and my hands and drags us off the dance floor. I look over my shoulder and wave to the guys as I stumble away to the ladies' room.

In the bathroom, Dayton hugs me and says, "Oh, my god, you were totally getting into it. See? I *told* you it's fun! We need to do this more often." I feel like we have our sync back. Her eyes crinkle as she talks, and I'm really happy to be here with her.

She moves to outline her lips in the mirror, while Bri inspects my makeup. Hers hasn't moved. I ask Bri how she does it.

"Girl, I hate looking like a melted doll," she replies. She looks pointedly at Dayton, who makes kissy lips at her and rubs at the running mascara under her eyes. Leave it to Day to turn makeup smears into smoldering smoky eyes.

Bri laughs. "I'm just sayin'. So I use all waterproof makeup and don't move too much."

She paints some pink lip gloss on me. "There, see? How cute is that?"

I purse my lips in the mirror and try to decide if it really is cute or looks like I fell face first onto a pink-frosted cake and forgot to wipe my mouth. I wobble a bit on my heels as I try to lean closer to the mirror for a detailed look. I decide I don't want to look that close.

"Good enough!" I say. "Let's go!"

Dayton grins, hugs me and Bri, and grabs my hand. We leave the bathroom and run to the dance floor.

"Woo-hoo!" she yells as the three of us dance with one another. Dayton dances like a wild child, hair flying, sweating, and moving with total abandon. She looks like she doesn't have a care in the world.

I realize I don't either. I haven't thought about soccer, tests, homework, or volunteer work since we got here. I close my eyes and turn and step to the beat.

The music pounds, and we join in the chant from the crowd, raising our arms toward the neon ceiling.

"T-G-I-F! T-G-I-F!"

Two more drinks and 134 minutes later, all I can think is that some letters and numbers are really awesome.

⸭ ⸭ ⸭

The first thing I think on Saturday morning is that some letters and numbers really suck. I try to get my eyes to focus on the bright screen on my phone to turn off my six o'clock alarm. My mouth feels like I ate a cashmere sweater, and the sugary smoke smell from the club is all over me.

Dayton groans from under a pile of blankets at the other end of her rec room floor. Bri is still asleep, uncovered and snoring softly in between us. I check her face. True to her word, her makeup still hasn't moved—except for the fake eyelash strip that is stuck on her cheek.

My feet are kind of sore from dancing in heels all night. I crawl around Bri to Dayton's side since I'm not sure that my head can handle standing yet.

"Hey, Day. I gotta go." I pat her shoulder.

Dayton grunts and rolls over, smiling groggily. She leans up on one arm, clearing her throat until she can finally talk.

"Hey." Her voice is scratchy. She rubs her eyes and checks the time on her phone. "Seriously? You're leaving already? It's only six."

"Yeah. I've got hours of homework and stuff for Service Club. I also want to work on my video for the club recruiting review. Which reminds me, have you—?"

She holds up a hand. "Don't start, okay? Please? It's too early to think. My brain is still asleep."

She glances over at Bri and smiles again. "I'm really glad you came. It was awesome, right? You wanna go out again this Friday?"

"I don't know. I'll check my schedule."

"Cool." She looks disappointed, but she gives me a hug and then burrows back under the blankets.

On my way out of the rec room, I pass between a mirror and a life-size cardboard stand-up of Krystina in her UNC uniform in the hall. I remember it from a huge party her parents threw when Krys finished her first season at UNC. I stand behind cardboard Krys and try to put my head over the shoulder to see how I would look in Tar Heels blue.

The reflection in the mirror just makes it look like Krys has two heads. Two heads may not be that far from reality. I remember Dayton's mom joking that the cutout was a good investment because they could use it again when Dayton made the team. All they'd have to do was replace the face part.

I may be lucky 8, but Day's the lucky one.

▦ ▦ ▦

When I get home, it's just me and my cat, Kitty Blaze, since my parents are on an anniversary trip. I flop on my bed to read my chemistry book.

The next thing I know, I'm waking up with book creases on my forehead. I'm so tired. Then I remember Nita's lecture and head to the kitchen to get some food fuel.

While I finish a somewhat healthy breakfast of a whole wheat English muffin and turkey bacon, I fast-forward through the clips that I've collected for the recruiting video. I find lots of shots that show me and Dayton playing for the Copperheads last year. There's the sync.

I also notice I have some pretty good passes to some of the other team players. I like watching myself set up shots for Nita, Lacy Sheridan (Nita's best friend and another forward on the Copperheads team), and others until I see my lame instep kicks.

My brain just won't focus, and I yawn a lot. I stop and end up on the Internet watching honey badger–Snow White mashups, Channing Tatum movie clips, and even less useful stuff.

When I finally head to the bathroom to shower, the first thing I noticed in the mirror was my bright pink lips. They totally clash with my Copperheads sweatshirt.

Ew.

chapter 7

o my relief, Dayton manages to make the
varsity team. The sync is safe.

When I ask Dayton at lunch how she
feels about the first game, she just shrugs.
"It's just another game," she says. "Just like
all the others we've ever played." I feel a
distance stretching between us, so I grasp for
something to say that'll interest her.

"Well, are you excited for the recruiting
review?"

She raises her eyebrows and her eyes open wide. "Oh, crap. That's today too?"

"Uh, *yeah*. How could you forget? They're going to highlight Nita's video."

"I don't think I can make it. Bri and I are going to watch the boys' game and go study at the library for our world history test."

Dayton has been spending more time with Bri after practice. They have some classes together, and I'm always doing homework or a Service Club meeting. And they party together.

For a moment, I feel a pang of jealousy, but my concern for Dayton washes it away. She'll miss out on one of the most important things we'll do this year. If I ask how far she's gotten on her video, she'll just change the subject.

"It'll be okay," I say, patting her arm. "Your parents have been through this before, and whatever they did with Krys worked. I'll take notes, and you can read them."

Dayton gives me a sad, little smile. "You're a great friend, you know that?"

▦ ▦ ▦

As the Copperheads run laps around the field warming up before our first game, my stomach sinks. No Dayton. I drop back beside Bri, who lags at the back of the pack.

"Do you know if Day's coming?"

"Oh, I'm sure she is. The guys are playing right after us," says Bri, sidestepping a puddle. I resist the urge to run full tilt through it and drench her.

"Oh, right. Yeah, she'll be here." I sprint and catch up with Nita and Lacy toward the front of the group.

"So what do you guys think about Lake Mary High?" I ask. "Who has a trout for a mascot?"

Nita runs her hands though her dark, blue-tipped hair. "They're just okay, but I still think it'll be up to us in front to be on it. Other than Alyssa in goal, defense is pretty weak this year. We need to keep the game to the other half of the field. Shouldn't be a problem though. We have some pretty good forwards this year. Right, Lacy?"

Lacy nods and looks down at her knees as

we run. She's working on coming back from an injury, and I wonder how she feels about Nita's plan. They're best friends, but Nita can be pretty intense.

As we round the last corner, Dayton shows up, trudging along. She's still doing laps when the rest of us break into groups to practice passing and shooting. In the past, Dayton would catch up and run alongside whoever was up front. Not today.

When she finishes and comes onto the field, Bri and I go to talk to her, but the whistle is blown. Coach Berg gathers us for the pregame talk. Dayton, Bri, and I all get to start. Dayton stares off into space as we take our positions.

We take possession at kickoff, Nita dribbling the ball straight forward. She feints right, preparing to chip the ball up and over an opposing midfielder to Lacy. The Lake Mary defenders turn up the heat. They close in around her, and she struggles to retain the ball.

Lacy is lagging behind her, so Nita looks to the right for Dayton, who's lagging too, but she catches up. When Dayton gets the ball, she stops for a second and then sprints forward with it. Instead of taking a shot on goal when she has the chance, she passes it back to Nita, who takes the shot. Nita nails it hard, but the ball bounces off a defender's thigh and back into play.

Nita yells something along the lines of "Unnnh," makes fists, and follows the Trout with the ball back toward the centerline.

I'm ready for her. When the Trout tries to boot the ball over me, I jump up and trap it with my chest. Wincing, I let it fall to my feet where I can control it.

I look up the field and see a mass of Lake Mary aqua-colored jerseys advancing. Behind them I see Dayton, unguarded, with only one defender between her and the goal. I know I can't get the ball through all of that aqua. It needs a serious power boot to get high enough up and far enough forward.

"Bri!" I have to yell to get her attention because she's staring off field from her spot at right D. She snaps back to the game. I pass it back to her, shouting, "Send it!"

Bri's kick is insane when she remembers to use it. Luckily, she gets it and sends the ball right to Day. Day stops it and then dribbles slowly and looks around instead of charging for the goal.

"Take the shot! Take the shot!" Coach Berg yells from the sidelines.

But she doesn't. She passes the ball to Nita, who is in front of the goal but buried under defenders again. We lose possession, and Lake Mary runs the ball up the outside edge of the field toward our goal.

The rest of the first half seems to repeat this. I run up and down the field, up and down. I stop the ball, steal it, and move it to the forwards. We lose it if I give it to Dayton or Lacy. Dayton moves like a slug and gives the ball away. Lacy is moving like an old lady. She's probably still worried about her injured knee. I finally start sending it to Nita every time.

"Sub!" yells Coach Berg on a throw-in. "Dayton, Lacy, Maddie, off the field! Nita— *play your position!*"

We run off the turf. I'm so tired that I'm

panting. Once I finally catch my breath, I turn to Dayton, who is sipping her water.

"*What* is going on out there, Day?"

"What do you mean?"

"Nita's plan only seems to work when I pass the ball to her," I say, straightening my shin guard.

"I didn't know she had a *plan*," says Dayton. "I thought we're just *playing*."

"Okay, but why do you keep giving the ball away?" I shake my head as sweat dribbles in my eyes. "You could have had lots of shots."

She shrugs, looking away. "I don't know. I thought Nita could have them." She stretches and looks at me. "Jeez, Mad Dog, you look really whupped."

"Yeah, that'll happen when you run all over the field playing *both* offense and defense. When you play center mid, you don't get a chance to stop and wait for someone to give you something."

"I want to hear more talking out there," says Coach Berg, coming over to us. "Good job passing, Madison. Pick it up, Dayton.

You're holding back. You don't always have to pass the ball to Nita, no matter how hungry she seems for it. You can score too."

After Coach Berg puts us all back in during the second half, Dayton starts missing the passes I send her. She's moving really slow, like a soccer zombie. My frustration is growing even though Nita has scored and the other team can't get past us to even put a shot on goal.

Then the guys' team shows up on the field next to us, and suddenly the sync is back on. Dayton runs to intercept the ball, takes shots, and just looks more enthusiastic. She even scores a goal. When we are back on the sidelines, she spends a good amount of time eyeballing the boys. But at least she was watching the game and rooting for our team. She even joins in the "Copperheads! Number One!" chant that starts when we win.

Coach Berg focuses his postgame talk on being hungry for a victory.

"We *are* the number one team to beat this season. That means we have targets on our backs. Even though we won, you weren't the well-oiled machine I expected to see. I want every gear doing its job and working with the other parts to move the machine forward, so we don't get hit."

Buzzkill.

Afterward, Dayton doesn't even say good-bye to me as she and Bri leave the locker room. *If we're winners, why do I feel like such a loser?*

chapter 8

osing is all in how you look at it," says Marta at the second recruiting review night. "Don't worry too much about it. It's a team effort, but you can still have some great moves as an individual no matter the outcome of the game. It's even better if you get those moves on video."

Nita and I shuffle uncomfortably on the hard chairs set up in the local YMCA gym. Marta shows her highlight video and goes over the good points. She compiled and edited it herself to have a relevant example of how a great video should look. It was also to pay Nita back for coming to talk to us underclassmen.

"Remember: Family, school, soccer practice, games, and training and recruiting," says Marta. "Those are your priorities if you really want to do D-I." She pulls out the pyramid again. My eyes focus on the word *friends* underneath all the other items.

While Marta talks, I feel my toes curl in my shoes. How can I show my notes to Dayton? She already thinks that I spend too much time on soccer and not enough on her.

Then I clench my hand. This isn't a problem for players whose friends are also serious about the top of the pyramid.

"Most of you know that recruiters don't really watch high school games. But I have it on good authority that at least one Division I coach will be visiting the area for other reasons. He may drop by a couple of high school games during division or regional finals to watch some candidates." She nods at Nita, who looks surprised. At the break, Nita and I hit the refreshment table.

"Did you hear?" she says, taking tiny bites of a carrot stick. "The WPS league has suspended play. I wonder what'll happen next in women's soccer? Both Alex Morgan and Hope Solo are going to Seattle now to play for the Sounders in the W-League. I'm bummed they aren't on this coast anymore. Having them near made it feel like playing pro isn't impossible."

I'm silent because I can't think of anything to add. I never even considered that I'd be good enough for a professional career. I don't want to play outside of college. It just never figured into my vision of the future. Then I come up with something.

"Maybe you should *go* to the University of Washington in Seattle. Then you can watch their games. Maybe even try out for the Sounders?"

"Huh. Yeah. Hope Solo went to Washington U. That was when she switched from forward to keeper. And Seattle's totally a soccer town. I like that, Mad Dog!"

Nita helps me make a list of stuff I still have to do for recruiting. Then Marta returns to the front of the room.

"Please turn in your videos. We'll get back to you with comments before the next review. Oh, and I forgot to introduce my assistants, Erik and Mark." She points, and we all turn to see the two guys waving from the back of the room.

I almost drop my notebook. Erik is the guy I danced with at Sugar Mill.

Division I hopes: RIP.

chapter 9

Dayton's always been lazy about returning calls and texts, but it never mattered before. We were together all the time. Now her parents have her working with a tutor during lunch. With all of my homework and studying on weekends, we have no time together except for soccer.

Practice isn't really good as "hang out" time, and Dayton is still a soccer zombie anyway. She's distant, doesn't talk much, and doesn't show much interest in soccer at all. Even around guys. Our sync is almost gone, and she spends most of her time waiting for the boys' team to run by. Occasionally, she puts in a little effort. But it doesn't stick.

I haven't found a chance to tell her about Erik and the recruiting review. She doesn't ask. When she doesn't show at all for practice one day, I'm not shocked. I'm terrified.

Did she quit? Where is she? When I ask, Bri has no clue either.

Even if Dayton wasn't into practice, she was at least *there* before. I feel naked on the field. I do okay, but that soccer sync feeling is missing. I don't have it with anyone else.

When I see Day at practice the next day, she says she's fine, that she didn't feel well, and that she's just been so busy she needed a break to catch up on sleep.

I totally get it. I give her a hug, and she hugs me back and sighs.

Twenty-two minutes into our game against the Springville Cardinals, Becca Miller is at left forward, dribbling, head down. I spot a Cardinal-colored blur speeding toward her from the right.

"Man on! Man on!" I yell, and Becca finally looks up.

The Cardinal defender tries to jab the ball, but Becca pulls an outside cut and shimmies around her, and then crosses the ball. Nita hammers in the cross, and we are at 1–0.

"Nita, you have *got* to teach me to do an instep kick like yours!" I gush as we run back to the centerline.

"It's not too hard. You just have to practice to make it automatic. It's all muscle memory." She nods to Dayton, who has stopped in the center circle with her. "You need some instep kick tutoring too?"

Dayton smiles half heartedly. And then we arrange ourselves for the next kickoff.

As the game progresses, Dayton passes off most balls I give her. I fight years of the sick sync habit and start sending them to Nita,

Lacy, or even Becca. Still, Dayton's presence on the field comforts me, and she's not totally useless. Occasionally, Dayton has a good steal. One time, she even takes a shot on goal. She sends off a weak grass cutter that the keeper easily dispatches.

Nita, on the other hand, takes every chance she can get. At one point in the second half, she has the ball and a defender on her. Nita moves as if she's going to kick the ball back to the midfielders. But at the last second, she scoops her foot in front of it in an awkward angle with her toe pointing in. She taps the ball back behind her, turns, breaks away from the defender, and gets a shot away. The Springville keeper catches it, but the Cruyff turn has everyone buzzing on the sidelines for the rest of the game. We beat Springfield 3–1.

Nita, Lacy, and I are the last people in the locker room after the game. I am about to leave when I hear an excited squeal on the other side of the lockers.

I swing my head around the end of the lockers because my legs are too tired to actually walk around. Lacy and Nita are sitting on the bench, hovering over something.

"What's going on?"

"Hey, Mad Dog. Check it out." Lacy hands me a stack of brightly colored brochures and forms. It takes me a second to realize that they're Nita's invites to summer academies and camps. I force my legs to move me to their bench.

I sift through the stack in awe. Nita's invited to UNC College Bound Players Academy *and* Duke Soccer School. She has invites to multiple camps in California and Arizona and even one at the University of Washington. Unbelievable.

"This is such a great pile!" Lacy says.

"Invites to things that'll cost a pile of *money*," says Nita, frowning. I hand her the stack and sit next to her. She's been on a scholarship from our soccer club, and I know money is tight for her.

"Yeah, they're expensive," I say. "But at least your invites are serious. And they'd be worth it. You've gotta be on all these programs' must-see lists. You know they just can't tell you that yet. I got some invites too, but I'm not sure if the coaches even know if I exist. Maybe I should dye my hair like yours," I say, flicking the blue tips of her hair. She lets a tiny smile break through.

"Look," I continue, flipping through the pile. "One is from UW in Seattle. You can go try it out and get that much closer to the Sounders. Maybe you should switch hair color to purple and gold."

The wheels turn in my head. And then I get an idea. Or two.

"We're going to celebrate!" I say, whopping the pile on the bench. "I think you should honor this pile of invites. I know a couple of players can use some inspiration right now. I'm going to have a team slumber party! In the meantime, I could really use a change of luck. How exactly did you dye your hair blue?"

chapter 10

My hair color now matches my middle name because it's a sign of good luck. In fact, it's the lucky color. Rockin' red hair makes me feel bold and in charge. I've come up with a "new luck" plan, including repairing my sync with Dayton on and off the field.

The slumber party was supposed to help Dayton remember the fun of soccer, but all she does is slump on the family room couch next to Bri. We're rewatching the NCAA women's soccer finals from a few months back saved on my DVR. Even though Stanford beat Duke to win the title, everyone else is having a great time.

Nita's like our sports commentator, giving out team stats as we watch. I learn more about college soccer in the first half of the game than I've ever known.

"I feel like a little kid," Bri whispers to me and Day. "Let's go out and hang with some mature people." Dayton sits up straighter and smiles at me.

"Not everyone, just us," says Day. "We'll tell them we're tired, go to your room, and sneak out the side window. They'll never know. And we can go have some fun."

I want to tell her I *am* having fun, but I also want to repair the sync. Badly.

In not too much time, Nita and Lacy are looking sleepy anyway. "They're probably in bed by nine most nights," Bri snickers. When I slide down the drainpipe outside my window and land on my butt outside the rec room, I'm not thinking about having fun. I'm sneaking out of my *own* slumber party when I'd rather be talking to Nita about college recruiting.

I'm dreading what would happen if Nita finds out. She could tell my parents and coaches. But what worries me more is what she would think of me as a teammate. I'm not thrilled, and I'm tired of Dayton avoiding soccer, but I do it anyway.

We climb into my dad's Escalade. I leave the headlights off until we get around the corner.

"You treat us right, Maddie," sighs Dayton, sinking back into the leather seat. She roots through her bag to pull out a small box of Frankenberry cereal.

"I do." We pull out of my neighborhood and head toward Raleigh. "But let's get one thing straight. If you guys get in trouble, we lose two good players. That can't happen, so I'm designated driver tonight. I loaded my English reading on my phone, so I can get something done while I'm busy *not* drinking."

Bri pretends to stare intently at her compact as she glosses her lips. She waves her hand over it like it's a crystal ball. "I can see my future, my immediate future, my future *tonight*. And it involves some guy. Tall, dark, and handsome, I think."

"Really? OTH again? Whatever happened to that PM frat guy?" asks Dayton.

I feel like I'm listening in on a private conversation. They have a language all their own and a whole history over the last few months that I can't share. "I didn't follow any of that," I say.

"I asked her if she's on the hunt again, and what about the premed fraternity guy she was into last week? Ooh! I need ice cream! Does Dairy Queen have a drive-through?" Dayton has polished off her box of cereal and is looking longingly out the window.

After a stop at Dairy Queen, we finally make it to the club. The bouncer recognizes Day and Bri and doesn't even bother asking for our IDs. Instead, he decides to talk to us. I'm relieved, since my hair is now a totally different color than Jennifer Nishito, college student. When he leans over, I try not to gag on his thick cologne.

"So I've seen you ladies around a lot. What you do for work? Must be somethin' hard based on all the steam you two blow off all week." He gestures to Bri and Day.

Dayton shakes her hair back and hits him with a high-wattage smile. "We work in a candle store at the mall in Fraser. Our boss, Nita, is a total pain in the butt, you know?" I'm as impressed with her skill as a liar as I am uncomfortable with it.

He smiles, nodding. "Figured it was somethin' like that. Well, you ladies have a good night." He waves us in.

We order drinks, and I feel like a totally different person than the last time I was here. I'm not impressed. I'm not into it. And I'm desperately hoping Erik isn't here. We claim a table on the second level. The noise isn't as bad up here, and I might be able to read in peace.

Two guys approach and try to talk to us over the music. They introduce themselves, and I try not to laugh. Day and Bri went out to be mature, and we are talking to high school guys.

The short, blond guy notices the soccer ball screensaver on my phone and asks if we play. Dayton suddenly finds a tear in the vinyl of the chair very interesting. As I nod and start to answer, the other guy breaks in.

"You guys play too? Hell, yeah! Who do you play for?" He has dark hair, and I look over to see Bri checking him out with interest.

"We play for the Fraser Copperheads," she says, smiling coyly and spinning one of her curls around a finger. *Really?*

"Copperheads! Snake girls. Ssss-sweet." He leers at her.

"Sssseriously?" I ask. What a loser. But he and Bri are already on their way to the dance floor.

Dayton is laughing so hard that beer comes out her nose. For a moment, I feel that sync again as I offer her the napkin from my Pepsi. She wipes down, and as she finishes, she shrugs and grabs the blond guy to head down to the dance floor, yelling, "I hope they play some TLC. I love nineties music!" As I watch Dayton and Bri twist and turn below, I wish they moved that fast on the soccer field.

I spend the night switching between reading and wondering when we can leave. By the time we get home and sneak back into my house, I know it's time to give my own goals some TLC.

chapter 11

The visit to Sugar Mill did nothing for the sync. Dayton's performance in practice—when she bothers to come at all—is still pretty weak. She seems to miss at least one practice a week and is usually tardy. I know Coach is on her case about it. When she's around, we barely talk, and I've stopped asking where she was or why she's late.

She's benched for one game and seems okay to be on the sidelines. It means less time together on the field. But I don't notice the difference as much as I thought I would.

I never paid that much attention to other players' styles, but with Dayton being in and out, I am. I change my own play based on what I see. I notice that Lacy at left forward still tends to hang back. As striker, Ruth Middleton is the person most likely to get yellow-carded. Becca Miller is a good striker too, but she's so overeager that she's becoming the queen of offside. I think twice before passing her a ball.

My new plan includes working on juggling and instep kicking skills with Nita after soccer practice. She's aggressive and a ball hog, which just forces me to try harder.

Today we play the Pickford Panthers. We have fewer players due to injuries, and Coach doesn't let Dayton start. As I lace up my cleats, I try not to think of how tough it's going to be.

After kickoff, I feel the training with Nita doing the trick. I slide the ball around Pickford defenders like a Twinkie on its way to

Dayton's stomach. We keep the pressure on. But without enough subs, we're getting tired.

My legs are weak by the time Coach finally subs me out. I stand next to Nita, whose eyes are shifting from the field to the stands and back again.

"See that guy in the blue jacket over there?" she asks. "That's the recruiting coordinator for UNC."

My heart thumps. I tell Dayton, and she just looks bored. Maybe she's pissed that she hasn't been on the field yet. I go back to Nita.

"We're wearing out, but at least we're ahead because of your goal," I say. Nita nods and swallows hard as we watch our team try to keep an edge over the Panthers.

I was cooled off, but I actually start to sweat again *before* I'm put back in. The score's stalled at 1–0. Knowing that there is a recruiter watching combined with a worn-out team worries me. But knowing that I have no sync to show him makes me *panic*. I have some good passes, but I'm still freaked.

Then coach puts Dayton in. I sigh with

relief. After Nita tries a header that fails, I intercept the keeper's short punt, jumping to trap it with my thigh. I pass it to Dayton, who runs it to the goal. And then she hesitates. That little pause gives a Panther defender enough time to challenge her. They spin and turn each other around as the defender tries for the ball. Dayton steps wide to . . . to do what? There's no good reason to leave the ball unguarded. As she does it, the defender plucks the ball, darts up the sidelines, and sends a floating cross to her forwards.

I give Day a questioning look, and she shrugs.

The other team gets the equalizer with a goal by their left forward.

After kickoff, Nita and Dayton give-and-go up the right side. As a Panther kicks the ball out of bounds, our right midfielder, Elise Heisel, runs to do the throw-in.

Dayton yells, "I'm open! I'm open!" As the ball comes at her, she puts her foot out. The ball whiffs over her laces straight to a Panther. It's like she's eight years old again—no control.

After that, I set up the ball only for Nita and Lacy to score.

Other players pass Dayton the ball, but she continues to miss perfect passes as the game goes on. She moves slowly and doesn't run to meet the ball. I'm exhausted from trying to make up for her lack of skill when the defenders who've been stealing from her try to get past me.

During the next attack, there's so much action around the box, it's hard to track all the shifting bodies and quick, super-short passes. I swear I see Dayton kick the ball with the outside of her foot to the nearest Panther. For a minute, I wonder if it's on purpose because she's looking right at the other player. The Panthers clear the ball, run it up the right side, and score.

When we lose, I am hollow inside. Nita looks like she wants to kill someone. Dayton looks unconcerned.

chapter 12

The human foot contains twenty-six bones. And right now, I want to kick Dayton with all of them. I head right home after the game to cool off.

An hour and a half later, I'm standing in the entryway of her house, struggling to hold back another rush of anger. The distance between us is now as far away as the goal is when you're playing D. You know it's there, and you can see it. But there's a lot of stuff between it and you.

"I just wanted to stop by to drop some things off. Like this," I say, handing her Jennifer Nishito's ID and the club clothes. "I don't think I'll be needing them anymore."

Dayton points to the rec room where her parents won't hear us talk. I follow her and notice that cardboard Krys has been moved into the rec room along with Day's soccer trophies. For someone trying so hard to avoid soccer, she's pretty much surrounded by it.

I don't want to sit, so I pace while Day stands next to cardboard Krys.

"You threw the game. Am I right?" I hold my breath.

She stares at me and misses a blink, but otherwise, she doesn't react.

Please say no. Please say no.

"Yes," she says, and I feel my world crumpling.

"Why would you do that? You knew how important it was. What's going on? I just want the truth. For once."

"Fine," she says. "I threw the game. I like to party more than I tell you, and I'm not doing ODP. I'm not playing this summer at all."

I take a deep breath before I ask, "Is it me?"

"No," she says. And then it's like I punctured a ball because a whole lot of stuff comes out.

"Maddie, you are who you are. And you *know* who you are and where you're going, and that's great. I don't know who I am anymore. I just know that *this*"—she points to cardboard Krys—"isn't me. I moved all this stuff out of my room so I wouldn't have to look at it.

"I know what Krys went through and what you're doing now, and it isn't worth it. There's so much pressure. Everyone around me expects so much—my mom, my dad, even *you*. The only time you want to talk to me lately is when you want to ask something about Krys or talk about soccer. No one cares what I want, and I don't want soccer anymore."

"But—"

"Oh, my god, aren't you listening? *I am sick of soccer!*" She throws out an arm and nearly decapitates cardboard Krys.

"God, tell me how you *really* feel!" I yell back. I instantly regret it because I don't want her to clam up again. I'm scared of being without her.

She sighs. "I'll tell you how I feel about soccer," Dayton says after a moment. "It's like one of those little tingles in the middle of your back. You get all twisted up trying to reach it, to scratch it, or poke it and make it stop. By the time you're done, you're just all twisted and messed up and don't remember why you reached for it in the first place. Every practice, every game since last fall, I had to decide if I was going to go or if it was the day I quit. I don't want another summer spent saying, 'I can't. I have soccer.' I'm out."

Sweat starts at my hairline, creeping down my head and over my back. *How am I supposed to feel? Everything is all jumbled together in my head. I had no idea I was part of the pressure. I feel guilty for that and sad that I didn't know enough to reach out and help her. How do we talk to each other after this? Do we talk at all?*

84

"Are you going to finish the Copperhead season?" I finally ask.

She shrugs. "I don't know. I've been kind of hoping I would get kicked off and wouldn't have to decide. The only reason I was doing it was to see you, but I kind of started hating it." She crosses her arms over her chest and looks at the ID. "And this means you aren't going out to party with me again, right?"

"I can't," I say. "I have soccer."

And I walk out of her house.

chapter 13

despite crying myself to sleep after arguing with Dayton, I go to school the next day. The puff under my eyes is fading, and I have a test in English.

Practice is Dayton free. I know without asking Coach or Bri that Day quit the Copperheads. I try to concentrate on the ball, but I miss my shots. A lot.

At the game against Greenridge, I just can't seem to concentrate. Nita takes the kickoff and passes it to Lacy. Defenders bunch around Lacy, but she manages to get the ball out to me. I cross the ball toward Nita, who chases it down and drives it into the net for our first goal.

Other than that first burst of good playing, I check out for most of the first half. Multiple times, I think about Dayton for a moment and mess up whatever I'm supposed to do next. I completely miss a pass from Elise. I don't hear someone yelling, "Man on!" I don't notice when Nita wants to do a crossover run. It's a good thing Greenridge is weak because I'm not helping the Copperheads much.

Another goal comes when Nita takes the ball, threads it through a clump of defenders, and tucks it neatly inside the near post. I clap, but I'm wishing I was somewhere else right now.

For the last half of the game, Coach puts in three other people in my position, using me as a sub. I'd be miserable if I wasn't so numb.

Coach Berg pulls me aside after the game. "I want you to remember that this is a whole team. Center mid has to be there for everyone. I think we're gonna see your leadership skills strengthen in the future. But right now, I see you letting one specific player affect your game. Right now, I'm rethinking having you start in the district finals. Work it out, get back in the game, and we can look at it again." He gives me a thumbs-up and walks away.

Crap.

⸬ ⸬ ⸬

On Saturday, I sit in my room petting Kitty Blaze, listening to music, and thinking. Thinking that maybe Dayton's right. Worrying about Division I soccer in addition to everything else the world throws at you is just too much.

My best friend is gone. My grades are slipping. The last score I got on the SAT practice test was lower than the first. Now Coach doesn't want to start me in the district finals where a Division I coach might stop by. I don't think things can get worse.

And then I get a message that Erik from the recruiting consultant's office has reviewed my video. There's a problem, and I need to call him.

Really? Really!

How do people do this? Maybe I'm just not good enough to play at the college level. And maybe I'm just not smart enough to get into a good school at all. Maybe Day has it right—do I even want to play college soccer?

Giving up on D-1 hopes seems like a really good idea right now. Then I can hang out more, worry less, and not have such a complicated life.

Might as well get started with the uncomplicating now. I pick up the phone. My stomach trembles when Erik answers. "This is Madison Wong. I got a message to talk to you about my recruiting video?"

"Hi, Madison. One sec, let me get your file."

Why does he need my file when he's obviously going to talk to me about underage partying?

"Oh, here it is." He clears his throat a few times like he is trying to buy time to think of what to say. "I reviewed your video, and there's something I'd like to discuss."

Crap, crap, crap.

"There are a lot of scenes of you and another player, this girl with the white-blonde hair?"

"That's Dayton." *Here it comes.*

"Almost every clip on this video is just you and her. You guys clearly did some of it outside of a game, but even the game videos are just you and her."

That's it? That's all? I wait for him to say more just to be sure.

"There are some great passes and footwork here. But to really make an impression, show some individual clips. Show some with other people besides Dayton. Variety is good. You can get more of that this summer during club ball and camps, right?"

I'm stunned. I feel like a huge weight just rolled off my shoulders.

"Madison?"

"Oh! Yeah, I'll get other footage. Uh . . . is there anything else?"

"No, that was the only problem I saw. Overall it's pretty decent. Just replace some of the clips and really stand alone and be independent."

I thank him and hang up. I'm flooded with relief and excitement again. It was pretty decent! *OMG.*

chapter 14

talking to Erik gave me the reality check I needed. It just isn't me to quit, so I decide to continue with my new plan. I have to catch up on everything I let slide when I was trying to make Dayton happy. Service to Seniors is over, so I put those hours into studying and training more with Nita.

"You gonna try out for the Region III ODP team?" she asks as we run through my neighborhood on Sunday.

"Yeah. Summer'll be crazy—club play, college soccer camps, and ODP. But I'm going to try."

"I wasn't sure you were. I was thinking you'd lost your mojo last week when Dayton quit. You were a mess out there. No offense."

"None taken. Everything I've ever done in soccer was with Dayton. I'm not sure how I am by myself. But I realized yesterday that reaching for D-1 has to go on—with or without her."

"Is that why you want to increase practice and training time with me?"

"Yeah. I want to work on some stuff. Like that instep kick. And I want to be in good enough shape that you won't compare me to a chocolate doughnut."

"I wouldn't call you that, chica. With that hair," she says, smiling and pointing to my lucky locks, "I'd probably call you strawberry cheesecake. And I think the cheesecake stands alone just fine."

▦ ▦ ▦

The work starts to pay off. My grades and practice SAT scores improve. I guess worrying about Dayton was really taking a toll on me. My confidence level increases.

Practice gets easier too. I can focus my thoughts on the rest of the game now instead of always looking for Dayton. My stomach threatens to get upset before each game when I realize I'm without the sync, but it goes away quicker each time.

As we play Yeopin Valley, I remind myself to look around for the best openings. If it's Lacy, I adjust my pass to compensate for her speed although she's getting faster. I know Nita can take it from the air, so I chip the ball to her. And I talk more on the field because I don't expect anyone to read my mind.

At the end of the second half, I get a pass from Elise and look to Nita, Lacy, and Becca, who's now playing right wing. All are covered by defenders. I'm not. The goalie for Yeopin Valley reads my movements and starts screaming at her sweeper, who does not want to leave Nita uncovered.

I crank my leg back for the kick and follow through with a blast of power behind my laces. The ball accelerates, and the keeper lunges, clapping her hands on thin air as the ball passes through her gloves. But she had come forward out of the goal, and I can't hide my disappointment as the ball smacks the upright and bounces back to her.

We win the game, but I'm still disappointed.

"That was a pretty good shot, Mad Dog," says Nita afterward. "You've really boosted your kick."

Practices, games, and training with Nita take up all the time I'm not using to study or research colleges. But I'm excited to take steps closer to a good Division I school.

"I like the work you're putting in lately," Coach tells me right before our game against Ironwood. "Your passing is getting more accurate. Your footwork is tighter. Good focus on offense. Just don't forget to move back if the ball gets past you. You play defense too."

I remember Coach's words, and play up and back. The benefit of conditioning training with Nita is revealed as I realize I'm not overly tired even though I'm running more.

When I get the ball at the beginning of the second half, I check the field. Ironwood is another weak team, which gives me a chance to try some strategy.

"Bri!" I yell as I play the ball back to her. "Look at Lacy!" Bri boots the ball way up across the field to the left. It's a risky move, but it works. Ironwood wasn't expecting me to send a ball backward, much less across the field. Lacy corrals it and carries it in alone, easily scoring a goal.

After we win, Bri comes up to me. "Hey, thanks for helping us out on D more and sending me that ball. I know we haven't talked much since Dayton quit. I stopped going out with her. It was just too much, you know? It was like she had something to prove. It stopped being fun. But I miss her."

"I miss her too. I'm not mad at her now. Just sad."

Despite my improvement, I still don't start in the first district playoff game. But at least I play.

And then Coach Berg tells me I'll start in the district final.

chapter 15

s I scan the crowded stands at the district finals game, I wonder who might be a recruiter. I feel totally excited and totally sick at the same time. I never pictured being here without Dayton.

"You ready to win this?" Nita says, coming up next to me.

"Yup. Higby's tough. You keep the pressure up front. I'll be there, but defense will need a lot of support this game."

"You're so good with the ball now. You might even give me a run for MVP."

"I don't think so," I reply with a smile.

"Me either," she says, laughing as she dodges my half-hearted kick at her shin. "But seriously, I heard a couple of people talking about nominating you for MVP at the end of the season."

Once the game is on, we are *on*. Nita easily weaves between the defenders of Higby High. I'm always there when the ball comes my way. I have sick sync with almost anyone I pass to. Lacy moves faster, and Bri is totally in the game.

By the middle of the second half, we're tied 1–1. I get the ball and see a Higby defender coming right for me. She doesn't hide that she's going to foul me. I pass the ball at the last second and brace myself for the smack of her lowered shoulder. And then I'm on the ground, shaky but still in one piece.

We get a free kick, and Coach Berg calls for me to take it. As I place the ball, I look around for teammates I can move it toward while the Higby players set up a three-player wall in front of me. Suddenly, I see a different opportunity. I realize I can do this by myself. There's no need for sync.

I feel the pressure building. I back up and then run to the ball. Keeping my toe down and my ankle locked, I kick through the middle of the ball. This time, the instep kick works—it clears the Higby wall and heads straight for the upper-right corner of the goal. The goalie stretches out but can't touch it. The ball rockets past her gloves and into the net.

It's a goal, and it's all mine!

As I high-five Nita and run back to my position, I look up and see Dayton in the stands. She gives me a hesitant smile and a little wave. She looks happy where she is, and I'm definitely happy where I am. I smile back at her and then turn back to the game.

We finish with a 2–1 win, and I know that I'm responsible for the game-winning goal.

And I did it alone.

After the game, I'm shocked when Dayton catches me outside the locker room.

"Hey," I say, not sure what else to say.

"Hey. So I was wondering if you might be able to help me?" she asks, eyes crinkling as she smiles. "I have to write a newspaper story for an assignment in English. I was wondering if I could interview you as if I'm writing a sports article. You know, since you're like the big star and everything."

I think for a moment before I reply. She looks really happy. Hopeful, even. I'm momentarily suspicious.

"We don't have to do it at a bar or dance club, do we?"

"Nope. I'm done with that. But it probably will involve Krispy Kremes and Cheerwine."

"Let's have strawberry cheesecake, too," I say, really smiling. "I'm kind of into that now."

We leave together like old times, and I feel something I haven't felt for a while. Looks like we're heading for a different kind of sync.

chapter 13

y whole life is a series of letters and numbers.

ENG II and CHEM I are tolerable. I could be the MVP, and I might make the Region III ODP Team.

I am Mad Dog, Maddie, 8, and number 26. I'm a Premier Level U-17 Fleet Foot. I am CM. I am a Fraser Copperhead. And we are number 1.

about the author

AMANDA HUMANN IS A
WRITER LIVING IN SEATTLE.
SHE LIKES RAIN, SALMON,
AND BEING SLEEPLESS, BUT
SHE DOESN'T DRINK COFFEE
OR CHASE VAMPIRES.

COUNTERATTACK

archenemy

As a defender for Fraser High, Addie used to be ready for anything. But now the biggest threat on the field is her former best friend.

the beast

When a concussion takes Alyssa out of the lineup, her rising-star teammate Becca takes over in goal. Will Alyssa heal in time for playoffs? And how far will she go to reclaim the goalie jersey?

blow out

Lacy spent the winter recovering from a knee injury that still gives her nightmares. Now Raven is going after her starting spot. Can Lacy get past her fears and play the way she used to?

offside

It might be crazy, but Faith has a crush on her coach. Can she keep her head in the game? And when Faith's frenemy Caitlyn decides that Faith's getting special treatment, will Faith become an outcast?

out of sync

Since childhood, Madison and Dayton have had soccer sync. But lately, Dayton is more interested in partying than playing soccer. Can Maddie get through to her best friend?

under pressure

Taking "performance supplements" makes Elise feel great, and lately she's been playing like a powerhouse. But will it last? How long can she keep the pills a secret?